Butts and Mutts

written and illustrated by
Anja Schubert

To the little humans and furry canines who brighten my days and amuse me endlessly.

5 years ago. Down in the sewers.

The **STENCH** of **poo** filled George's nostrils as he swept the sieve through the river. A dirty nappy, then a broken barbie doll floated past him. But then, oh Joy!

He stretched out his arms. There was an apple bobbing right next to them! Perfect for lunch. George barely noticed his foot slipping. Seconds later his face broke the murky surface of the water, a big **POO** sat on his head like a crown.

"Seriously?" yelled George into the darkness. He shook the *POO* off his head and watched it escape downstream.

Worried about the time he scooted after the escaping apple and scooped the fruit into his now full bag. The masters would be pleased with him, at least today. But soon he would be in charge, and then the World would pay for making him swim in this **stinky POO** river every day. He was meant for greater things.

Chapter 1

Present Day - First day of school

Bettie danced through the school yard. Strands of blonde locks had escaped her pigtails and snaked their way into her bright blue eyes. The bell sounded as her dainty foot hit the first step before the classroom.

Just in time! Thought Bettie as she pushed the door open. She dropped her bag and coat into her locker and quickly took her seat. The teacher was nowhere to be seen.

I wonder where Miss Crabapple has got to? She thought. Not one to be distracted Bettie got out her school books and neatly placed them on her side of the desk. She glanced at the empty space beside her.

Maybe next year I'll have a desk buddy? Bettie smiled sweetly at the other children as they brawled in, pushing and shoving each other as they half destroyed the tidy room. She spotted Billy over in the corner pouring what she hoped was apple juice into another student's bag. But knowing Billy she thought it was probably **PEE**. She stole another glance at the container and noted the weird smell crawling through the room. Yep. Definitely pee. He was getting soft. Bettie remembered how Billy had put a bee hive in a school bag last summer. Bettie remembered well because the bees had been pretty angry when she'd dropped her maths book on them. Her cheeks flushed at the upsetting memory.

Before she could arrange her pens a massive trumpeting noise erupted from Billy's corner.

Matthias rose from his seat and pointed an accusing finger "Billy just **FARTED**!" screamed Matthias.

"Billy!" The teacher's voice fell on the room like a wet blanket.

Students stopped mid throw, confused eyes stared first at Billy and then at the front of the room. Miss Crabapple had walked into the room, a small, dishevelled child wearing a baggy shirt and shorts in tow.

"Billy! See me after class." said Miss as she wrote Billy's name on the blackboard in perfect cursive.

The ultimate sign of doom.

"Everyone please take your seats." said Miss Crabapple and waited a minute until everyone had sat down. The room was now full of squirming feet, and

writhing hands, falling pens and shuffling papers. Apart

from Bettie, who sat perfectly still, hands folded neatly on her lap.

"Right then students." Miss Crabapple gently nudged the newcomer forwards. "This is Vee. A new student from out of town." She smiled oddly as she looked around the room for an empty desk. "Ah. That'll do. Vee you can sit with Bettie. Bettie please show Vee around at recess." Said Miss.

Bettie **beamed**. "Of course Miss!" said Bettie, she'd never been picked to show a new kid around before. There was muffled giggling from around the room. Miss shot the class a sour look.

Vee sat down and shot Bettie a real stink eye. *"I don't like you, you're all pink! Stay away from me or else."* said Vee and leaned away from Bettie.

Betties' heart sank and at that moment Vee did a little FART, but no one seemed to notice.

Chapter 2

Playground tantrums

Bettie felt sick. She'd never *not* done what a teacher

had asked. But it was clear the new kid didn't want her around. Vee had gone off to a corner of the playground with a tub of yoghurt and asked to be left alone, leaving Bettie to sit on the bench under the big tree like she did every other day, trying her best not to get **pooped** on by the pigeons fighting above.

Bettie was biting into a cheese stick when Billy walked up. She sighed. *Right on time.*

"Hi Billy." said Bettie in a quiet voice.

Billy glared at her half eaten cheese-stick. "Give me your lunch dork." said Billy.

Bettie's stomach growled. She was *really* hungry. She considered saying no. But it would cause too much trouble. Bettie smiled and held out her lunch.

"Here. Enjoy." she said.

Billy snatched the bag of chips and salad roll and ran off. As he did his butt erupted in a concert of toots and hoots. Just loud enough to cause the other kids to laugh and point.

At least he left me the cheese stick. Bettie finished off her tiny lunch and then pulled out a book from her bag and started reading.

A shadow fell over her. She looked up into the frowning face of Vee.

"What was that about?" asked Vee.

Bettie shrugged. "Billy was hungry. So I gave him my lunch." she said.

"Does Billy get hungry every day?" asked Vee.

"Pretty much." said Bettie

"That **SUCKS**." said Vee.

Bettie's eyes opened wide and she gasped. "Oh my gosh! You can't say that Vee!"

Vee grinned. *"Sucks?"*

"Stop it! We'll get in trouble." said Bettie.

"What? Vacuums SUCK, *bugs* **SUCK**, *you suck a lollipop. Perfectly good word, sucks."*

Bettie laughed.

"Here". Vee pushed half a ham sandwich at her. *"Eat it. You're weak looking."* said Vee.

here.

Bettie looked into the serious face surrounded by a wild head of hair that reminded her of a tumbling weed. It even had a few leaves in it. She thought she spotted a twig behind one ear. Graciously she accepted the food from the newcomer. She *was* very hungry.

"Why do you put up with him?" asked Vee.

Crumbs flew from Bettie's mouth. "Oh him. He's

not the worst." she said.

"*There's others?*" asked Vee.

Bettie's eyes shone. "Oh yes. Lots. Almost all the kids really, some of the grown-ups too. Miss Crabapple is ok though. I mean *not* nice exactly but she doesn't openly make fun of me." said Bettie.

Vee seemed confused. "*But why? I mean, you're a really pretty girl, you dress nice, you have goldilocks hair and you smell like strawberries! I thought you'd be the most popular girl at school!*" Vee's eyes were fixed on a far away cloud. "*I thought you'd be mean to me.*" said Vee quietly.

Bettie stuffed the rest of the sandwich in her face and shrugged. "Is that why you said you don't like me?" asked Bettie.

Vee patted her on the shoulder. "*Yeah. Sorry. I know what it's like getting bullied for being different. It's hard being the new kid and stuff.*" said Vee.

"That's ok!" Bettie's smile spread from ear to ear. "Maybe we could be friends!"

Vee grinned. "*Sure. Stranger things have happened.*" Vee stopped to scratch a really itchy itch just above the left butt cheek. "*You shouldn't put up* with those bullies." said Vee and looked down at the cherubic face of Bettie beaming back.

Bettie went quiet and looked around making sure no one heard them. "It would be too dangerous to do anything." she said.

Vee's nose crinkled, then strong arms folded across a mud splattered shirt. A declaration was made. "I'm here now! I'll be your backup! Together we'll get them!" cried Vee.

Bettie's shiny blue eyes turned to steel and a tiny hand rested on Vee's arm. "No Vee. I meant it would be too dangerous for *them*."

Chapter 3

A secret revealed

Bettie danced over the bricks beneath her pointed toes, oblivious to the tolling bell. Who cared if she was only just on time? Who cared if the teacher didn't spy her there ten minutes early. She looked across at Vee, striding along beside her.

Bettie had never had a friend like Vee before. Strong, chaotic and loud, yet quiet at times. Vee could go from being silently absorbed in a drawing to halfway up a tree in the blink of an eye. Belching the alphabet, fart fights, butt scratching and snot rivers smeared in sleeves were all part of Vee's charm. Bettie liked to use a tissue of course, it wouldn't do to ruin a perfectly good outfit with snot.

A long **FART** erupted from beside her. Bettie giggled so hard she almost peed her pants! "Vee!

That's so **GROSS**! We have to get inside." said Bettie.

Vee snorted a snot bubble back up a grubby nose and nodded sagely. *"Of course, chief. Whatever you say."* Vee gave Bettie a salute.

Rolling her eyes Bettie forged ahead. There was learning to be done!

Lunchtime came around again. For weeks Vee had stood by Bettie and no one had come to claim her lunch, no one had tried to give her a **wedgie** or a **NOOGIE** or a swirlie turd bath. Life was good.

"I gotta go pee." said Vee.

Bettie went to rise to tag along but her friend stopped her. *"All good, I'll be back in a jiffy."* said Vee and ran off towards the toilet blocks, Bettie was left looking at her box of juice and wondering what clouds were made of.

She drank the juice, and waited some more. She noticed a cloud that looked a little bit rude. Where was Vee? Hopefully it wasn't food poisoning! She knew that ham shouldn't have been green!

Alarmed Bettie leapt to her feet and ran over to the toilets. She could hear raised voices from the disabled toilets.

*"Get off me you **skid-mark**!"* cried Vee.
Vee's voice!!! And it sounded like trouble! Bettie's pulse quickened, her hair seemed to rise around her as if in a strong wind. Her fingers clenched in small fists as she pushed open the toilet door. Static filled the air.

Billy and his goons had cornered Vee. By the looks of the black eye and split lip on one of them it seemed Vee had put up quite a fight. Vee was being held upside down, pants hanging by one leg, screaming and kicking, head perched over the toilet bowl. A red mist descended into Bettie's eyes. How **DARE** they do this to her friend!? Rage exploded in her heart and she released years of bottled up frustration and tears all at once.

The explosion was massive.

Vee sat dumbfounded on the floor.

Billy and his goons lay crumpled in a heap, in front of the toilets.

PANTSLESS.

Their underpants were on show for all to see! There were skid marks on all of them! Kids stood around the bullies pointing, laughing and cheering as the group scrambled hastily to recover their pants. As they made their escape they **ROOT-TOOT-TOOTED** with every step.

Bettie used the distraction to help Vee off the floor and pulled up the oversized shorts that had fallen off before the other kids noticed.

Vee stood stunned, mouth open like a trout. Bettie gently led them out and to the side, avoiding anyone spotting them.

Bettie handed her drink bottle to Vee.

Vee, still resembling a fish, gratefully accepted the water and took a big sip. *"Thanks."* said Vee.

"No problem." said Bettie and nervously glanced around. *Gods I hope no one saw us!*

Vee plonked onto the grass and let off a **BIG fart**. *"Ohhhhhh. That's better! Been keeping that one in for a while!"* said Vee.

Bettie giggled. "Better out than in?"

"You bet." Vee's eyes locked with hers. *"So. You're a superhero."* said Vee.

"What!?" Bettie watched the rain of spittle fly from her mouth, *darn it, that's not very lady-like* she thought. "I don't know what you're talking about."

"You've got some sort of super power." said Vee and nodded. *"Yep, I think it has to do with pants."* Bettie's eye's said that wasn't quite right. *"Oh boy! It's farts! You can make people* **FART***! Holy* **poop** *cakes. And how!"* declared Vee smiling.

Bettie's eyes darted around in a panic. "Please keep your voice down Vee!" she said.

Vee smirked. *"Only if you come clean!"* said Vee.

Licking her lips nervously Bettie sat down. "I wouldn't call it a super power. But I have made

some strange things happen. **AWFUL** things.
DANGEROUS things." said Bettie.

Vee's eyes lit up. *"Oh!? Tell me! I love a good story."*

Bettie was about to launch into the tale of her drunk uncle Jimmy and how he ended up pooping in a lawn chair, falling out of a very high oak tree and going to hospital in an ambulance without pants on. But then the World turned yellow.

"**GAH**!" Bettie fumbled at the thing sticking to her face.

"Here let me" Vee pulled the flier off. *"Huh. Look at this."* said Vee.

"It's some kind of job ad?" Bettie read out loud. *"Sick of the daily grind? Why not grind up some humans and help me destroy the World? Only serious henchmen must apply, health and dental plans not existent. You probably won't live long enough to need them."*

Bettie scratched her nose. "Must be some sort of joke." she said.

Vee didn't think so. *"Have you heard the rumours about Big G?"*

"The rapper from the UK?" asked Bettie.

"No that's the Big P. He's been banned from

performing here. My parents wouldn't tell me why, they just offered me ice cream. I love ice cream so I took it. Asking where I came from works the same."Vee laughed. "But seriously, I think we should find out who wrote this."said Vee.

"Why?" asked Bettie.

"So we can defeat the bad guy! Duh!" said Vee, grinning.

"I... I don't think that's a good idea." said Bettie.

Vee had already bounded off. "C'mon! We have to get you ready!"yelled Vee.

Bettie jumped to her feet and started running. "What do you mean!?" asked Bettie.

Vee grinned, "I think you'd look great in a cape."

Chapter 4

A hero is dressed

"I look ridiculous." said Bettie.

"You look **GREAT**. Though I'm not sure about the shoes." said Vee.

"The shoes make this outfit." said Bettie.

"They're not exactly Health and Safety compliant are they?" Vee thought.

"What do you mean?" asked Bettie looking at her feet.

"I mean, you don't see crime fighters facing down mobs wearing sparkly pink ballet flats. What if something heavy falls on your feet and the criminals get away?" said Vee.

"This is stupid." said Bettie tugging at her clothes.

"Put these on." Vee pushed a pair of heavy black boots into Bettie's hands.

"What are these? They smell like a toilet." said Bettie.

"I use these when I go help the mad woman on the hill with scooping up cow **PATTIES**." said Vee.

"Eew! These are covered in cow **POO**?" Bettie wrinkled her nose in disgust.

"Not just cow **poo**. Put them on." said Vee.

"Maybe.. I'll think about it." said Bettie.

"Do you need the tutu? Super-heroes tend to be

more stream-lined don't they?" Said Vee.

"The tutu stays." said Bettie.

"And the tiara? Won't that fall off?" asked Vee.

"The tiara is **ESSENTIAL**." Bettie wouldn't compromise on it.

"And the glittery tights? Why are they SO pink? They're not exactly stealthy?" said Vee.

Bettie huffed. "Look. I said this was stupid. But if you insist that I fight crime or whatever I at least want to look good doing it. And superman wore bright blue and red pants, so he wasn't stealthy either."

"You have a point. But you have to wear boots. For safety." said Vee.

Bettie grumbled as she slipped her feet into the stinking boots. "Fine." She propped up. "How do I look?" she asked.

"**Amazing**. They won't know what hit them." Vee threw something in the air. "Catch!" yelled Vee.

Bettie ducked just in time. "What on Earth Vee!? What was that?" said Bettie.

"A tomato." replied Vee.

"It's all **SQUISHY**. Oh no it's all over the bed

linen!" She sniffed the air, gagging. "Is this rotten?" asked Bettie.

"You hardly expect me to throw perfectly good food at you do you?" said Vee.

"Why are you throwing anything at me??" asked Bettie.

"Reflexes." said Vee.

"What?" Bettie was confused.

"Need to hone your reflexes." said Vee.

"What for?" asked Bettie.

"In case you face ninjas?" said Vee.

"Is that likely?" Bettie wasn't sure about this.

"Maybe? Yes? Definitely. There will be ninjas." said Vee, nodding.

"We don't even know if there really is an evil mastermind. The flier was probably a joke." said Bettie.

"One way to find out." said Vee.

"How's that?" asked Bettie.

"The mad woman on the hill." said Vee.

"Jane Hatter? The dog-walker? The one that lives in that tiny shack?" asked Bettie.

"Yup!" said Vee.

"How would she know?" asked Bettie.

"Oh she knows stuff, she's always mumbling to herself about secrets and weapons and stuff. You know, while we're out collecting poo. Not just cow patties either, there's dog **POO,** chicken **poo**, roo **poo**. And of course the composting toilet needs emptying

once a month." said Vee.

Bettie needed to process this, she was quite possibly standing in the poopiest shoes on Earth. And they were on her beautiful pink rug.

"What does she do with all that poo?" asked Bettie as she desperately looked around to check for **poo** stains.

"I never asked. Mainly I just help cart the poo to the big metal hatch in the side of the hill and it slides down some sort of tunnel thing." said Vee.

"There's a hatch in the hill?! How could someone who lives in a dirty little shack afford to create a chute into a hill? And why would they fill it with **poo**!?" asked Bettie.

Vee scratched an itch, the thing seemed to move around, first up an arm then down a leg. "Dunno. I never asked." The itch had reached an ear somehow. "Maybe she enjoys the rustic and cosy atmosphere of a mid-century wooden construct?" said Vee.

Ah yes. The child of real estate agents. They could sell a beat up van as a one bedroom fixer upper with a potential for beautiful views.

"Ok." said Bettie.

"*Ok what?*" Vee now had an index finger up a nostril, finally the itch was cornered.

"We go see the mad Hatter?" said Bettie.

"*Oh, right, we're expected for tea there around eleven tomorrow.*" said Vee.

"What!" Bettie couldn't believe it.

"*I talked to her this morning before I came round.*" said Vee.

"You did?" asked Bettie.

"*Yeah, I knew I'd get you to come round. Oh I got it!*" said Vee.

"What?" Bettie watched with a mix of amazement and horror as Vee extracted a large green blob on the end of a grubby finger and ate it.

"*The itch!*" said Vee.

Chapter 5

Jane "the Mad" Hatter

"Vee my favourite tiny human!" Vee fist-bumped the flurry of activity before them. Somehow the small woman was never still, two dogs seemed to create a ball of movement around her legs and she was constantly brushing the wild fringe of hair from her eyes.

"And who's this? The friend you mentioned?" asked the woman.

Vee nodded. *"This is Bettie."*

A gloved hand extended in an expectant fist. "Hi. I'm Doc Jane."

Bettie gently bumped the outstretched hand. "Nice to meet you ma'am." said Bettie wondering what kind of doctor Jane was.

Jane's strange laugh echoed over the open hill. It reminded Bettie of a sick duck having a coughing fit. "No one calls me ma'am. It's Jane to my friends. Or Doc. Some call me Dr. Hatter, and some call me mad!" Jane flashed her pearly white teeth. "Now, who wants tea?" She pointed at a small wooden table laid out with a white table cloth, it had pots of tea and pretty porcelain cups and plates of scones, sandwiches and other tasty delights.

Bettie's eyes lit up. "**WOW**, that's quite a

spread. Is that just for us?" she asked.

Jane smiled. "Is it? Of course it's for you. Sorry, I don't entertain much." She pulled out several chairs, the two balls of fur flying around her became still as they leapt into a chair each and looked at their plates expectantly. "Sausages," she addressed the dogs. "You'll have to wait until our guests are seated." The dogs shot her an unhappy look. "Just a minute I promise, we need to feed our guests first." Jane said to the two dogs.

Bettie watched Vee's face erupt in a grin.

"Oh. Please don't wait on my account." said Jane and smiled as she placed a burger and a scone on each of the small plates before the dogs.

Bettie had expected the dogs to wolf down the treats. She did **NOT** expect them to pick up a knife and fork.

"What the!?" Bettie exclaimed as she watched on.

Jane seemed panicked. "Sausages! You forget your manners!" she cried. The dogs quickly dropped their cutlery, looked at their owner for a short second and said

"**WOOF?**" The smaller one grabbed his treats in

his mouth and ran off. The other dog soon followed.

"Did they just use a knife and fork?" asked Bettie. She couldn't believe her own words in her ears. And it seemed as though Vee was just as surprised.

"Uhm. No?" Jane's eyes darted around in panic. "Scone? Cream? Home made jam!?" Jane was in a panic.

Bettie wasn't distracted by the tasty food. "I'm sure. How can they even hold a knife? They don't have thumbs!" She paused, thinking back. "Or do they?" she asked.

"Oh. Uh. Oh dear. Uhm. Busted?" defeat spread across the woman's face. "How about we have tea and then I'll explain. Yes. Might be for the best." said Jane and looked over to the bushes beside the shack where one of the dogs was eyeing her. "You may as well come back to the table sausage. I think the jig is up."

Chapter 6

Secrets, dogs and powers

They arrived in the cavern. Jane was nervously wringing her hands and Vee was running around making owl sounds. Bettie's eyes were wide trying to take in everything. There were dogs **EVERYWHERE**. They were pushing carts, walking around with clipboards and standing at water coolers having chats about space-time continuums. Some had lab coats on, some were just labs. Laurel and Hardy, the two original dogs, had detached themselves from Jane, put on name badges and now stood perfectly still behind her. They looked smarter, bigger, somehow a little **DANGEROUS**. Bettie was reminded of bodyguards.

"What is this place?" Bettie asked.

"Oh. Right. I promised to explain. Well you see. How do I put this." said Jane.

"As short as possible?" Vee quipped seemingly out of nowhere.

Jane took a deep breath. "I am the head of an

international organisation working to bring down evil geniuses who plan to destroy the **WORLD!**" said Jane.

"*Oh.*" said Vee.

"Right." said Bettie. "Is it related to this?" She held out the yellow flier.

Jane gasped as she read it. "Oh dear. Yes indeed. Oh dearie me. It's happening sooner than I expected. Oh dear! So much to do!" She pushed the kids towards the elevator they'd come in on. "I'm sorry tiny humans, you'll need to go, this is going to get dangerous fast."

"*We can help!*" piped up Vee.
Jane stopped briefly, not one familiar with the abilities of the average child she didn't question the offer. "Really? Well, that would be grand!"

"*You're convinced?*" Vee had expected more push back, adults generally underestimated children.

"You are sure of your abilities, yes?" asked Jane. The kids nodded.

"That's good enough for me! You'll need an escort each while on the base or you'll get lost." Jane nodded behind her. "Laurel and Hardy will make sure you get fitted out with equipment. I'll prepare a briefing in the dining room. There's no time to lose!

Welcome to operation prevent **POO STORM**!"

Bettie wondered what she'd gotten herself into as they were bustled off deeper into the underground bunker, down spiraling stairs and into a large metal room. There were weapons, armour and everything you might want to start a small war lining the walls.

Vee's face lit up. *"Cool!"*

Bettie was horrified, so many dangerous things! She thought of the safety boots in her backpack, *good choice Vee.* "We don't really need weapons do we?" asked Bettie.

A cold nose nudged Bettie's shoulder. It was Hardy.

"Sure you do. Spikey George is as dangerous as they get. Here-" before Bettie could get over the talking dog she was looking at the thing he'd thrust at her. "**This**. Is a mark II super wetter. It will rain a heavy tranquilising spray on your enemy from up to two meters away, rendering them unconscious in only five minutes." The dog grabbed something else off the wall, it was long, black and shiny, there were multiple grips. "**This**. Is a stick. You hit people on the head with it. Depending on how hard you hit them they may hit you back or go to sleep." Hardy wheezed. "Possibly forever. **HA. HA**." he said.

Bettie was shocked. "I don't need weapons thank you. I have my own methods." she said.

"Oh? And those would be -" Hardy was interrupted by the intercom.

"Uhm. Yes, hi. Everyone ok? Oh dear, if you

could please finish up and come to the dining room? That would be grand. Uhm. Thanks. Bye." there was a rustling. "Where's that button. Why do I never find it." More rustling, something fell off the desk. "Oh there it -" Jane's voice cut off.

Vee giggled. *"Our fearless leader huh?"*

Laurel coughed as Hardy growled. "She's tougher than she seems. Now get dressed -" he pointed at a rack of army fatigues.

Bettie raised her hand "Sorry Mr. Hardy? I brought my own outfit, if that's ok?" she asked.

Hardy sniffed her briefly, there was something different about this small human. "Sure. Whatever you like. Both of you hurry up. We need to be back upstairs. **ASAP**." he said.

Bettie raised her hand again. "What does that mean?" she asked.

Hardy slapped a paw on his forehead. "It means get a wriggle on! We're already late!"

Chapter 7

The Plan

"WOW." said Hardy.

Bettie felt Hardy scan her up and down. "Just wow. So **THIS** is what you'll be wearing to take down the most dangerous criminal the World has ever seen?" he asked.

Bettie could see Vee suppressing a laugh out of the corner of her eye. She knew she looked fabulous, it wasn't her fault no one else seemed to share her love of fashion. And pink. She did **LOVE** pink. And Glitter! With a burst of confidence Bettie thrust her hands onto her hips, raised her chin high and said. "Yes!" said Bettie.

"Hm." Hardy scratched his chin. "I hope that secret weapon you've been hiding is something special. Time to go, humans."

The dining room was huge. Scratch that. It was enormous. **GINORMOUS** even. Jane stood at the end of the biggest table Bettie had ever seen. There were dogs in uniform, dogs with clipboards, dogs pushing around whiteboards with complicated symbols. There were biscuits.

Vee's pushed up the visor on her storm helmet. *"May I have a biscuit?"* asked Vee. The visor fell down again. Vee now resembled a stack of laundry with a bowling ball on top.

The room stopped. All eyes focussed on them. Bettie adjusted the small, pink mask slipping down her nose.

Jane smiled. "Of course! Have as many as you like!" Her eyes rested briefly on the glittery pink Bettie, her brain didn't seem to know what to do with the information it was given. "Uh - I see you're ready to go! Excellent. I'll run you through what we know so far." Jane pulled over a large whiteboard. On it were the word "SEWERAGE PLANT" and the yellow flier Vee and Bettie had found.

Jane pointed at the words. "So, we know the sewerage plant is somehow involved. We've seen George's minion's come and go at all hours."

Bettie was confused. "Who's George?"

Jane glanced up. "Oh. Did I not say? Oh. Dearie me, I think I missed a bit. Rewind!"

A dog with a different whiteboard came along. This one had a large photo of a lizard wearing tailored trousers on it, many bits of red string, and newspaper articles stuck all over it.

"That's better." Jane whipped out a long stick.

"This-" She pointed to the lizard, "is George. Also known as Spiky George, Big G, Trouser George, George the Evil, and for some reason George the **poo** scooper. He does tend to kill anyone who calls him that though. He has made it known that he plans to destroy the city and eventually rule the World."

Vee stuck up a hand.

Jane gave Vee a nod.

"Why is the Lizard wearing pants?" asked Vee.

Jane rummaged through some papers on the table. "Excellent question! The answer is — we don't know. But he always wears pants. Even when swimming!"

Vee thought about this. *"Interesting."* and cast a knowing look Bettie's way. *"Maybe it's where he gets his power?"* asked Vee.

Jane looked confused. "Like **MAGIC** pants?" she ruffled through the papers again. "Uhm, I don't think he has magic powers, mainly just lots and lots of henchmen?"

Vee's bum itched, and a good scratch followed. *"How does he get them to do what he wants?"*

"Uhm." Jane's eyes rolled to the ceiling. "Money, blackmail, promise of cheese? Usually enough to bend the will of men, women, or rats. Though I haven't ruled out electronic mind control." said Jane.

"So what's our plan?" asked Bettie, she could tell Vee was getting impatient, and itchier by the minute.

"Oh. Well we need to investigate the sewerage plant." said Doc Jane.

"That's it?" asked Bettie.

"Uhm. It's the only lead we have, hopefully we find more there. I've been training the dogs as fast as I can, but they're not great at stealth." said Jane.

"We'll handle it!" Vee's voice screamed from within the dark helmet.

"We will?" Bettie wasn't so sure.

"Yes! We've got this! Between my ninja skills and Bettie's superpowers those goons don't stand a chance!" said Vee.

Bettie looked at her friend in surprise. "Ninja skills?" she asked.

Vee smiled. "I took up Karate a few years ago. You know. For self defence."

"Oh." said Bettie.

Hardy had placed a paw on Bettie's shoulder.

"Wait. You have **SUPERPOWERS**?" he exclaimed.

Vee flicked open the helmet visor. *"Of course she does! Why else would she have her* **SUPERHERO** *outfit on?!"* said Vee.

Jane smiled from across the room. "Makes sense to me!" She adjusted her glasses. "What IS your superpower exactly?"

Vee was grinning.

Bettie turned the colour of a cherry.

"I can **BLOW PEOPLE'S PANTS OFF!**" said Bettie.

Jane's eyes locked with hers. "I see. Exactly HOW do you do that?"

Bettie shuffled her feet. "I can make people fart. Really BIG farts." she said.

"I knew it." Vee mumbled.

"**FASCINATING**." Jane started taking notes. "How powerful is it?"

"I once made uncle Jimmy clear the family pool and land on top of an oak tree." said Bettie.

"How **BIG** was this tree?" asked Doc.

You could hear a pin drop in the silence.

"Grandma says her Grandpa planted it." said

Bettie.

Jane's eyes looked like saucers. "How many houses high would you say it was Bettie?"

Bettie thought about it. "Oh, about five or six I guess?"

Jane made some hasty scribbles. Murmured to herself then announced. "**WOW**. Oh. **WOWZERS**. By my calculations, you can turn people into ***giant fart bazookas***!"

Bettie shrugged. Vee was all smiles. And then the alarm went off.

Chapter 8

The Evil Genius prepares

Big G admired his reflection in the floor to ceiling mirror. I look *magnificent*. He turned around so he could see the cut of the trousers. *Brilliant, perfect fit around the tail.*

"I'll take three pairs." said Big G.

A small man, with shiny flat hair and a very round head hurried over. A tape measure was hung around his neck. "Of course sir. May I suggest the new Italian wool pin-stripe sir? It's oh so fine."

George looked down at the sniveling figure of the tailor. "*Italian? ITALIAN?! I only wear BRITISH wool. I AM A GENTLEMAN you useless bag of WORM DROPPINGS!* Get out of my sight! I want those other pants tomorrow. I'll keep these on. And remember. British!" screamed George.

The tailor, **confused** but too scared to say more,

hurried out of the room. He had never met a giant talking Lizard before. And certainly in his wildest dreams wouldn't have imagined making pants for one! He glanced behind him. Maybe it was time to move to New Zealand.

"Mr G. Your car is ready." said the new arrival.

George finished adjusting his braces. A clean, crisp shirt and blue cravat finished off his look. *Yes, he thought. Exactly like a refined English gentleman. No more* GEORGE MCPOO *pants. No more George the turd fisher!*

He turned to his number one henchman. "Are the new rats ready Mr. Fluffballs?" asked Big G.

The large ball of fur nodded. "Their brain implants were tested this morning. Good to go Mr G."

"And the EXPLOSIVES?" asked George.

"Almost all of them are done. Just waiting on the nerd to finish the last two devices, then we can place them in the sewerage plant. Should have those by the end of the day." said Mr Fluffballs.

"Excellent!" said George, he was pleased. Soon. Soon they would all know what it was like to walk through a river of toilet juice. What it was like to spend your days knee deep in turds and reeking like the butt end of a butt. He looked around for his number two. "Where's Mr. Sumo?" he asked.

Mr Fluffballs looked up from his phone. "He's out back boss." he said.

George grabbed his coat and headed to the door. "Well get him! What's he doing back there that's so important?"

Fluffballs shrugged. "He had lunch so I suppose now he's cleaning his **butthole**?" he answered matter-of-factly.

George sighed. Bloody cats, such disgusting creatures, they had no elegance or refinement. And that unnatural obsession with licking their buttholes. **YUCK**. He'd have to get them some pants.

"Mr. Fluffballs. Stay here, get yourself and that gross brother of yours some pants." said George.

"Pants boss?" asked the cat.

"I'm sick of seeing your butt holes all the time. Cover up or find a new job." said George.

Fluffball was a coward by nature, and his brother was an idiot. No one else would give them a job. There were limited employment opportunities for lab experiments gone wrong. Fluffball watched his boss get in the black limousine and drive off. He took a quick look at his **butt**. What was his issue? He hurried to his brother.

"Hey Bro, is there something wrong with my butthole?" He pushed his fluffy **BUTT** into the other cat's face.

Sumo inspected the region slowly, and with

care. "Nah, looks perfect Bro. Check mine?" The cats swapped over.

"Pristine Bro. Good job on the clean." Sumo beamed. "Thanks Bro!"

Fluffball gave him the bad news about the pants. Sumo took it well. "Oh no worries Bro. We'll look top notch! I've got some ideas!"

The tailor didn't know what hit him. He'd never had to order in parachute material before. And he'd certainly never crafted pants with so many studs before, or a special flap for, as the fluffy gentleman put it - *butthole cleaning.* Definitely time to move to New Zealand. Or possibly Holland, he'd heard the tulips were nice there.

Chapter 9

My Ass

"This is my **ASS**." said Doc Jane.
The kids sniggered.

Jane cocked her head. "My **ASS** is called Carl." said Jane.

Vee snorted so hard a big snot bubble nearly hit Bettie.

Jane looked at the wild donkey with affection and gave him a carrot. "It's important to feed an **Ass** well, or they get tummy troubles." Carl's beady red eyes seemed to say – I'll do anything for a carrot.

Bettie had tears streaming down her cheeks, and Vee was in hysterics. *"Do you ever have to pick up* **POOP** *from your* **ASS**?" Vee snorted and huffed.

"Well of course, otherwise there'd be Ass **POO** everywhere." Jane gave Carl another carrot after he bit her hand. "Are you quite alright children?" Concern was written all over her face. She fished out a bandaid for her bleeding finger. And another carrot for Carl.

Bettie put a steadying hand on Vee as she doubled over. "Sorry Miss Jane." Bettie wiped the tears from her face. *"That IS a very lovely Ass you have there."* said Vee.

Vee exploded and ended up rolling on the ground unable to control the screams.

Bettie tried to calm herself. "So. Carl. What does he do?" she asked.

Jane smiled. "Transport. Nothing like a big strong **ASS** to get you from A to B."

The kids needed a minute.

"Now where'd I put your shoes? There's a good **ASS**." wondered Jane, and then after some searching brought out the bunny slippers.

The kids needed another minute.

There were unanswered questions buzzing through Bettie's head.
How could a Lizard be taking over the World?
Why did he wear pants?
Why could dogs use cutlery?

And talk? And where did all the poo go!?

Jane promised answers on their return. There was no time to lose. They would need to ride through the underground tunnels.

FAST.

Bettie held on for dear life as Carl bounded through the darkness. A powerful miner's torch showing him the way. Vee, sat behind her with one arm around her waist, was Hooting with joy as sticky threads of spittle lashed past them from Carl's mouth.

"**GROOOOOOOOOOOOOSSSSSSSSSSSSSS**!" Vee yelled with glee.

"Shhhh. We need to be quiet!" Bettie worried their enemies would hear them coming.

They rode on in silence, Carl's feet, encased in their pink bunny slippers, barely made a sound.

Carl slowed down.

"What's up boy?" Bettie whispered.

The donkey stopped and bit Bettie on the leg.

"**OW**!" Bettie turned to her friend. "I think we need to get off." Vee slid off over the donkey's **BUTT**, grabbing Carl's tail on the way down. Carl snorted angrily and missed with a badly placed kick.

"*Ha ha!*" laughed Vee.

"Vee!" hissed Bettie. "Don't make our ride back angry! Give Carl a carrot and let's go." she said.

Vee grudgingly obliged, receiving a small bite as thanks.

The kids made their way along the tunnel and soon hit a tight bend. "I think this is it Vee!" said Bettie.

They squeezed through the gap and found themselves surrounded. By the stench of **POO**!

Vee coughed as their eyes teared up. *"Yep. We're definitely here alright. That's* **STINKY**! *"* said Vee.

Chapter 10

Face off

Bettie and Vee crept along the wall. They were looking for an evil lair, or an office, or even a bin, somewhere they'd find files. Vee had pointed out there might not be files. Bettie thought that was CRAZY. How else would the bad guys keep track of their expenditures for tax purposes? The only alternative was not paying tax, and that was ludicrous!

The deeper they went the worse the stench got! *We need to make this quick.* Bettie waved at Vee to hurry and started running.

CRASH !

Bettie bounced off a ball of fur and landed hard on her bottom. Vee skidded to a halt beside her.

Fluffballs was staring right at the kids, **SURPRISE** filling his yellow eyes. "What are you two meant to be eh? Oi Bro!" He called out. "Come an' look at this here."

Vee helped Bettie to her feet and they took up

what they thought was their scariest fighting stances. Vee slid comfortably straight into the Karate pose Kiba Dachi, while Bettie, less familiar with fighting of any sort stood on one leg and put her fists on her hips.

"Ha ha!" Sumo peeked around the corner. "Cute kids. Are they dinner?"

The colour drained from Bettie's face. "You'd better watch out or..." said Bettie.

"Or what kid?" asked Sumo.
Vee launched at the cats with a flying side-kick. And was slapped down mid-air.

"*What!?*" said Vee, surprised.

"Huh huh." Fluffballs chuckled. "Cute little tasty ninja huh?"Bettie stood motionless.
Again Vee launched a blazing attack, the tiny form whirling through the air like a spinning top, feet and hands like spears. Sumo stuck out his staff and jammed Vee against the wall.

"Not bad kid. But we're a bit bigger and a **LOT** meaner! Ha ha!" said Sumo as he turned to Bettie.

"And what do you do Princess? Look pretty?" he asked.

The cats both laughed hard.

Bettie looked at the crumpled form of Vee. "Yes.

I do. And that's not a bad thing!" she screamed. Her eyes rolled back, she took a deep breath and she FOCUSED.

BLAAAARRRRTTT!

The explosion of **FARTS** was like a pair of jet engines going off. The cats were launched screaming into the air by their butts going nuts. Sumo was catapulted into the ceiling and Fluffballs was carried off into the dark.

Bettie grabbed Vee by the hand and pointed at the cat stuck in the ceiling. "Time to make that scumbag talk!" yelled Bettie.

Vee grinned and wiped the blood from a busted lip. *"My pleasure!"*

Bettie watched as Vee leapt and **SPUN, SLAPPING AND KICKING** the now trapped villain.

"What do you want?!" Howled the cat.

Bettie signaled to Vee. "Oh we didn't say?" she said.

"Nah Bro." said Mr Fluffballs.

"Sure?" asked Vee.

"I would have remembered Bro!" the muffled voice came through the ceiling.

"Oh. Sorry. We want to know how Big G plans to destroy the city please." asked Bettie.

"How do you know about that Bro?" There was panic in the cat's voice.

"Never you mind. Tell us or, I'll make your butt

REALLY **EXPLODE**." said Bettie.

"Anything but that Bro!" the cat squealed.

"All I know is right. There's a nerd who made us a bunch of explosives yeah? So we put them all over the place right? And then the boss sets 'em off right? **BOOM!** And the city sinks into the sewers Bro!"

Bettie gasped. Vee was getting ready to kick the villain again. She held out a hand to stop the tiny ninja. "Wait!" She walked closer to the cat, her cape flapped around her in the foul smelling wind. "Why does he want to destroy the city?" asked Bettie.

The cat shrugged. "Well, not exactly a secret Bro. It's because -"

Rats erupted from every corner. Their eyes blank, their faces limp and **FOUL SMELLING DROO**l dripping from their open mouths. They scurried as one towards the kids.

Vee's back pressed against Bettie's. *"Time to go!"* said Vee.

They rushed back the way they came, the wave of rats right on their heels. They'd almost reached the entry. Then a tiny clawed hand grabbed hold of Bettie's ankle.

Oh no.

Chapter 11

Boom Chakalaka

Tiny claws stretched out at them. Beady tiny eyes and gnawing teeth rushed at them.

Vee kicked at the rats rushing up at them

"*Bettie! Do something!! There's too many!*" yelled Vee.

Bettie concentrated. She concentrated hard. The front wave of rats stopped. The heads of the rats behind them smashing into the ~~butts~~ of those in front. *Just where I want you.*

The explosion.
Was.
Epic.

Hundreds of rats were flung into the air by the power of their own farts, wave after wave.

Bllaaaaaaaaaart!
Blaaaaart !
BLLLAARRRRRT!!!

Those just behind were pushed back by the stinking gases of their brother's and sister's butts.

But for some reason the rats kept coming. Bettie

was getting tired. Just before the rats got them a mouthful of **ROTTEN TEETH** grabbed her cape and she was dragged through the tunnel.

Vee hooted and yelled as Carl galloped through the dark and the rats were left far behind sitting in the smell of their own butt holes.

Bettie thought *'those hadn't been normal rats!'*

Dr Jane was in her lab. Staring at something green and blobby in a small glass tube.

GLOOP.

It seemed to do a flip.

Bettie would have been amazed, but it was hard to be surprised after a morning of talking dogs, ninja cats and zombie rats.

Jane glanced up. "**OH**! Children. You're back." She smiled. "What did you find out?"

Vee fell into a lab chair and started spinning around.

"Not much. We got attacked! By ninja cats and some weird rats." said Vee.

"Makes sense. Those are Big G's minions. We

expected they'd be there." said Jane.

Bettie's eyes went round. "We did!? You didn't tell us!" she said.

"Oh dear. Dearie me. Did I forget? I told someone." She bit her lip. "Who did I tell? Oh dear." She shot a finger up in the air. "I know! I told Carl." said Jane.

Bettie was not impressed. "You told your **Ass** about it?"

"I did!" said Doc.

"Your Ass that can't talk?" asked Vee.

Jane's lip pursed. "Of course my Ass can talk." she said.

"Carl can talk!? He didn't say **ANYTHING** to us!" said Bettie.

"Oh dear. He is rather shy." said Jane.

Vee spat across the room "**SHY**? *That evil, yellow toothed, mangy bucket of bones?!*" said Vee.

Jane nodded, "Oh yes, **PAINFULLY** shy. Apologies children, I should have told you as well. Looks like you went ok though?"

Bettie cleared her throat. "Well, we found out Big G has had his goons put explosives all over town. They plan to blow the whole lot tomorrow

and drop the city into the sewers!"

"Oh yes I knew about that." said Jane.

Bettie and Vee stared at the strange woman in her mud splattered lab coat.

"You did?" asked Vee.

"Oh yes." said Jane.

Vee's eyes narrowed. *"How did you know?"*

Jane smiled oddly. "Ah. Oh dear. Well, it's because I'm the one that made the bombs." said Jane.

"You what!?" the kids screamed in unison.

"I had to! Oh dear.." Jane wrung her hands and accidentally dropped the blob. "Oh **POOP**. That's going to **KILL** something." Doc reached for an empty jar and began chasing the now agitated blob around the floor. "I'll explain as soon as I've caught this little fellow. If you could wait outside for a minute? This thing *is* rather dangerous." She was half way under a table now as the blob tried to make its escape.

Bettie went to wait at the door when Vee grabbed her arm. *"Let's go."* said Vee.

"Jane asked us to wait." said Bettie.

Vee frowned. *"Jane is one of the bad guys! She just said so herself! Making bombs to blow up the city!"*

Bettie had tears in her eyes. "I suppose, but maybe she had a good reason?" she said.

"There's no good reason to build a bomb. C'mon. We'll stop these cabbage heads ourselves." said Vee and pushed Bettie towards the lift.

As they got to the top Vee grabbed their visitor passes and threw them down the shaft.

Bettie sighed. "I never even found out where all that **POO** goes."

Chapter 12

Vee shines

The bright green goop exploded all over Vee's face.

"Wow." breathed Bettie. "That was the

BIGGEST SNOT BUBBLE I've ever seen! Could be a World Record!"

Vee smirked and wiped the snot on a sleeve. *"You think? Awesome!"*

Bettie slapped her friend on the back. "Let's go home." she said.

Vee looked confused. *"Home? We haven't found Big G yet!"*

Bettie's feet slid to a stop. "We can't take him AND his goons on our own! Let's go home and tell our parents, they'll know what to do."

Vee snorted. *"Riiiight. Parents. Your parents have superpowers as well do they? 'Cos mine just sell* real estate."

"Of course not. They're parents. And we're just kids!" said Bettie.

"But you're a real-life superhero! And I'm a helluva side kick!" Vee's finger jutted at Bettie. "YOU need to face up to your destiny." said Vee.

"Really? Destiny?" asked Bettie.

"Yup." said Vee.

"You think we can do this?" Bettie wasn't sure.

Vee's confidence was infectious. "Absolutely. One hundred percent sure. Because if we don't stop Big G, everyone is doomed." said Vee.

Bettie adjusted her pigtails and straightened up a bit. "So everyone is counting on us?"

"Yup." said Vee.

"Alright. Let's do this." Bettie paused. "Wait, we don't know where he is!"

"Not yet, but find me a payphone and I can find out." said Vee.

Bettie's face scrunched up. "I have a mobile you can use." said Bettie.

"Your parents gave you your own mobile!?" asked Vee.

Bettie blushed. "Well, it's mainly for taking selfies for my blog, mainly."

"*You have a BLOG!?*" asked Vee.

"Uhm, yes, but only my parents can read it." said Bettie.

"*Can I read it?*" asked Vee.

"Sure! If you like, I can ask dad to add you, he's my sysadmin." said Bettie.

"*What's that?*" asked Vee.

"I *think* they're people who are meant to help you with your computer problems at work, but mainly dad yells at people a lot on the phone about forks and something called DNS and tells them to turn computers on and off a lot. And they add people to blogs." said Bettie.

Vee nodded sagely. "*Oh. That makes sense I guess. Cool. Phone please?*"

Bettie handed over the pink beauty that was her phone. Layers of pink, shrouded in pink glitter and pink sparkly stones and pink butterflies. It was an ode to pink.

Vee gingerly pressed the on button and typed in a number.

"Who are you calling?" asked Bettie,

"You'll see. Shh, it's ringing." said Vee.

A gruff voice answered. "Ullo? Who's that Bro?"

Bettie's mouth fell open.

Vee held a sleeve over the phone and put on a weird accent. "Elo? Bro? Dis is Bob. Bob and Bob?" said Vee oddly.

"There's two of you called Bob Bro? Bob and Bob?" asked the voice.

"Dis is right. Wee saw your ad in the yellow paper? We would like to apply for dis job?" said Vee.

"Cool Bro. You got your own weapons?"

"We has weapons. Big ones." said Vee.

"Cool cool. So, pay's fifty dollars per day, no dental, and if you die we keep the money Bro. Alright Bro?"

"Dis is cool. We are unlikely to die, wee are very strong and very mean. Where do wee go to start?" said Vee.

The cat seemed to think. "We got a big thing on tonight, FIVE pee-em, at the abandoned cat food factory. I'll bring the paperwork Bro and you can start

ASAP. Entry is through the red door."

"Very good. Wee see you later?" asked Vee.

"Cool Bro. Look forward to meeting you, you sound like a couple of tough dudes." the voice said.

The phone hung up.

Bettie couldn't believe it. "Vee that was **INCREDIBLE!**" exclaimed Bettie.

"It was, wasn't it?" Vee's face gleamed.

"Now what do we do?" asked Bettie.

"I think we need to hurry up and get the bus. I'm not keen on walking across the city!" said Vee.

The kids sat at the bus stop twiddling their thumbs. Twiddling the thumbs that were preparing to save the City! Nay, the World!

"We probably should have disguised ourselves." said Vee.

Bettie looked at her friend, who was still in head-to-toe oversized army gear. "We kind of are?" said Bettie. Bettie was still in her full hero glam. There had been some surprised looks from the other passengers.

"I meant so the bad guys don't recognise us!"

Bettie smiled. "Would our school uniforms do?"

"*Yeah I guess?*" said Vee.

Bettie grabbed her backpack. "I folded them up in the lab, and didn't want them getting covered in dog hair."

"*Cool!*" Vee started pulling the clothes over the big storm helmet. "*How do I look?*"

"**BULKY**?" said Bettie.

"*Excellent.*" said Vee.

"But you still have the helmet on." said Bettie.

"*Yup.*" answered Vee.

"I think they'll recognise you." said Bettie.

"*Really?*" asked Vee.

"Yes. I think I'll just stay as I am." said Bettie.

"*Ok.*" Vee paused, fidgeting in the now insane layers of clothing. Bettie noticed a strange red flush moving up the small neck.

"Sure you want to wear all that?" asked Bettie.

"*Uh. Maybe you can help me get the jumper off? It's getting hard to breathe.*" said Vee.

"Of course." said Bettie.

"Thanks." said Vee. The bus stopped a block up from the factory. They had about ten minutes to come up with a plan.

Chapter 13

The final boom

They didn't *really* have a plan. Bettiewas chewing on
her fingers, she kind of wished that crazy scientists or
at least some of her dogs were here. But Vee was
pretty insistent on the whole "Jane is evil" thing.

A large rusty red door loomed in front of them.

"So, crunch time!" Vee's massive grin reassured
Bettie.

"Yeah. So the plan is?" asked Bettie.

"Go in guns blazing!" exclaimed Vee.

"But we don't have any guns?" said Bettie.

Vee's nose scrunched up. *"Well, powers and legs
blazing then?"*

"Or, and it's just a thought, we sneak in quietly
and have a look around, see how many there are

and THEN blaze?" suggested Bettie.

"Yeah? I guess that's the sensible option?" said Vee sounding disappointed.

Bettie carefully slid open a crack in the door and looked through. "Coast seems clear, I think we're good to go." she said.

Vee nodded silently and followed Bettie into the gloom. They crept quietly along the dark shelves that seemed to run in all directions. A low murmur in the distance led them to the factory floor.

"Holy poo-cakes it's Jane!" yelled Vee.

Bettie clamped her hand over Vee's mouth as fast as she could. "Shhhh!" said Bettie.

Too late, the two dogs beside Jane's feet jerked up their heads and looked straight at them.

"Oh **POO**." Bettie felt dread in her stomach.

"Grngl grngl" said Vee through Bettie's fingers. The bigger dog looked up at Jane and they seemed to exchange words. Then the dogs returned their glares straight at the giant lizard lounging on a big gold throne.

Pew!

Blart!

Vee removed Bettie's hand and whispered *"Maybe they didn't see us?"*

Bettie shook her head. "They *definitely* saw us. There's something not right here. Why aren't they attacking us?" she asked.

Vee shrugged and pointed at the big board of dials and wires at the other side of the room. *"I reckon', that's the control center. We need to smash that thing up!"* said Vee.

Bettie followed Vee's finger. "You think so? It's a bit.. big? Dad's computer fits in my back-pack. Seems awfully over the top?"

Vee's head bobbed vigorously. *"It's how bad-guys do things. Haven't you read the pig-guy comics where he battles the evil Thunderdome?"*

Bettie said she hadn't.

"Well the control center in that looked just like that!" Vee squealed excitedly. This time some of the rats had heard them and ran towards them.

Bettie grabbed Vee's shoulder and turned to run, but they were met by a big wall of fur, set with steely red eyes. A blow to her head sent Bettie out cold, there would be no giant fart to save them this time.

Vee's eyes opened slowly. This was met with a sharp pain just behind the right eye. *"Oh poo".* Looking around Vee spotted Bettie, she was still unconscious, and tied up against a pole. Jane was standing by her, checking her head. Vee's face got hot when the scientist came over.

"*Get away from me!*" screamed Vee.

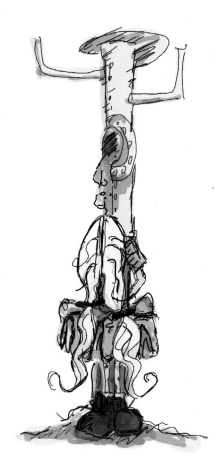

"Calm down .. erm.. *child!*" Jane pressed

something into Vee's hands while pretending to check the restraints. "Be still, and get ready to use this." Jane whispered into Vee's ear. "I've already untied Bettie, she'll come round soon."

Vee's eyes widened. Get ready how? Untied Bettie? What side was Jane on? Vee's confused eyes followed Jane back across the room as nimble fingers grasped the object from Jane.

"We're ready Big-G." Jane handed something to the lizard.

"Excellent Doctor.. uhm.. whatever your name is. Your children will be released as agreed." said the giant lizard.

Vee's eyebrows shot up. Children!? They had hostages!

Jane rushed over to a cardboard box beside the lizard's throne. "Oh thank-you Big-G!"

The lizard stomped a heavy foot on top of the box. "*After* we destroy the city."

Jane's face sunk. "But. We. I. You said." George's face split in a wide grin. "Things change my dear. Things change. And I'm not sure I trust you." he signaled to some rats to carry the box away.

Tears ran down Jane's face. "You. You

MONSTER." cried. Jane.

George laughed. "Oh yes. Blame me for your own failings as a mother." he looked over to Bettie and Vee. "I hope the dangerous one has been drugged enough so we can proceed with the operation?" he asked.

Jane nodded sadly.

"Good." George nodded to his main henchmen. "Time to activate the bombs!" he yelled. Fluffballs went over to a big red lever.

Jane raised her teary face. Her face split into a big grin. *"NOW!"* screamed Jane.

Silence.
Surprise.

BOOM.

The explosion was huge. Rats, cats and one evil lizard

flew through the room, smashing into walls, doors and the roof.

Bettie rose off the ground, her hair and cape flying around her. Her eyes were filled with a bright light. "Now Vee!" she yelled.

"What!?" asked Vee.

"Brace yourself!" said Bettie.

Bettie's hands rose and as the farts of a thousand rats filled the room Vee felt restraints fall away, then rose into the air and hovered next to Bettie.

"This is **AMAZING!!!**" yelled Vee.

"I can't hold you for long Vee. The last part is up to you!" Bettie hurled her friend at the Big Lizard, who had managed to get to an escape exit!

It all made sense now. Vee held out the syringe with firm hands and screamed a primal scream as George's scaly butt came closer and closer.

"What the - ?" George looked down as the syringe emptied itself into his left butt-cheek. His already heavy eyes caught a glimpse of Vee's triumphant face as he sank to the floor.

"Well done kidlets!!" Jane hurried across to

Vee and grabbed something from George's pants pocket.

"*What's that?*" asked Vee, trying to see.

"The mind controller!" said Bettie, who had sunk to the floor in the middle of the room. Exhausted Bettie flopped onto her back and cried "Poop! I'm done!" she said.

With the press of a single button Jane released the thousands of rats from George's control. She held the controller out to Vee. "If you would be so kind?" said Jane.

Vee grinned and smashed the electronic gadget with a mighty blow then ran to Bettie. "*We did it!! We saved the World!*" said Vee.

The kids rejoiced.

Jane coughed quietly. "Ahem... well... uhm.. not *quite*. Though you did save the town from a giant shower of **POO**. That would have been nasty. Some people may have died."

"**POO** rain?!" the kids chimed.

Jane laughed. "Oh yes. I made poo bombs. They had to be real explosives or I'd be found out, but I softened the effect by padding them with poo! Lots of poo."

"Gross. Why **POO**?" asked Bettie.

Jane didn't even pause to answer. "Lots of it around! And I had Vee to help me collect it!" Jane giggled."Sorry kids. I should have told you earlier. I modified the bombs so the town wouldn't be destroyed in case I couldn't come up with another plan in time. But then you guys showed up!"

Vee suddenly remembered the box. *"Oh my gosh! Where are your kids!?"*

Jane walked to the back of the room. "Ah yes, my *children. I'm sure they're fine.* " Jane emptied the box onto the ground.

Vee shrieked. *"Frogs!?"*
Jane smiled. "Genetically enhanced frogs. I've been teaching them karate!" She leaned down and scooped up the squirming green creatures.

"Come to mama widdle ones." cooed Doc.

Vee laughed. *"Ninja frogs. Pull the other one."*

Bettie elbowed her friend. "Talking dogs and ass remember?" she said.

*"Oh yeeeeahhhhh."*Vee's feet shuffled awkwardly. *"So what do we do now?"*asked Vee.

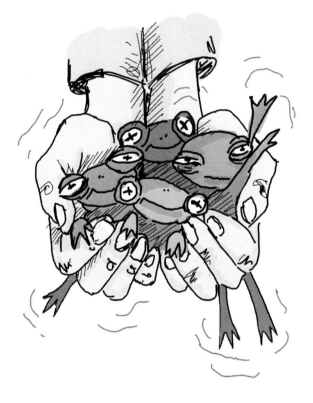

Jane looked up from her babies. "Clean up, deactivate the various explosives across the city. But the dogs can handle most of that." She seemed to remember something. "Oh! Well there *is* that super-villain in the next town planning to destroy the ozone layer and force us all to live under-ground. I could probably use some help there!"

The kids shared a knowing look. "We're in!" they

yelled,

Jane laughed. "*Fabulous*! The froglets will need a few years until they're able to fight evil. Best get on our way though, I vaguely remember he planned the rocket launch for tonight!" said Doc.

And with that a new crime-fighting duo was born. Many villains were beaten, crisis averted, a tiny kitten found a new home and mastered Kung-Fu. But those are stories for another day.

The end.

Made in United States
North Haven, CT
05 March 2023

33632260R00050